The demon looked down at Todd, his eyes full of flame, his teeth black, dripping with blood. This wasn't the first time that they had met, but it was the first time that the demon felt something...a chance to win.

You Don't Smile Enough.

"The single greatest insanity of mankind is the belief that another man can possibly understand what is happening in another man's mind, and that that man has any right to judge based on what insanities are playing out within his own. Psychology is a fraud."

This book is based on real events, mixed with personal opinion.

Chapter 1. *(The only Chapter.)*

It had been a tough week for Todd, a tough month, a tough year. His pointless, underpaying job, (baker at Publix,) had used and abused him for years, brainwashing him, as they did with all foolish enough to wear the green.

The land of the beautiful people…That's what Todd had come to call the green monster, Publix. Women, most teenage sluts fresh out of high school and eager to please, did as they wished, all eye candy for the perverse store manager, Joe, and his crotch pilot assistant manager, Bryce. They, these silly girls, all far too stupid to work anywhere else, were the spandex and G-string crew, all completely convinced that they were the next big thing, the next to get promoted, when all they really were…were tight little asses and big soft tits on display.

Behind the scenes, Todd, and countless others, the uglies, the ones truly making the store run, fought day and night, on the clock, and off the clock, the urge to quit, knowing deep down that there was no future for them within the hellish walls of the green mile. The fact that he, they, didn't walk right out the fucking door, was as close to a miracle as the world could produce. It was a hell, it truly was, a hopeless belief that one day…maybe, just maybe, things might get better, that all his, their hard work…might be noticed…but it never would be, not so long as there were teenage girls willing to wear spandex and G-strings to work.

On Friday, Sept 11th, 2004, 3 years after the NY attack, now a conspiracy freak holiday barely remembered for what it was, Todd was working his way through a fairly normal morning.

When…

"We need dinner rolls, 100 of them!" A voice, a girl's voice, demanded.

Turning around, Todd saw two of the stores most prolific bimbos, Tiffany and Christine, dumb and dumber, G-strings, tits and asses…future Publix managers…or so they believed, and our perverse overlord, Joe, allowed them to think, standing at the counter, tits nearly bursting out of their partially buttoned up shirts…as usual.

Both of these half-wits, Tiffany and Christine, were notorious cock suckers, legendary really, having been caught on their knees several times, once by our janitor who was quickly fired the next day then branded a thief. Both these girls would suck off anyone they believed might help their glorious careers…and this was one of those times…there were cocks to suck, and they were on a mission.

As it turned out, these nitwits had heard that one of our local radio stations was sending a news crew to our local firehouse. Believing this would be the perfect time to be seen…to get their knees a little dirty, potentially get themselves on television for a few seconds wearing their nametags and wide-open shirts, letting their puppies bark, they had quickly concocted a scheme to deliver an assortment of free merchandise to the firefighters…pretending to be completely unaware of the news crew when they got there.

"Ok," my less than genius asst bakery manager, Lisa, another product of big tits and little brains, replied, no clue as to the work required to carry out such a thing, as she had been a decorator for all of 4 months before her promotion and never baked a single thing.

The two girls walked away, their plan in the making, already working their throat muscles for a big afternoon of sucking.

Ten Minutes Later…

(I shit you not…10 minutes.)

I had just started the rolls…frozen, out of the freezer, on pans.

Now for those of you ignorant to the world of baking, 100 dinner rolls, 3 pans in total, to do them right, would take, at least, an hour, maybe more, but only if that was

ALL that you were baking.

They were not at all the only project I had going at 6:30 in the morning…hardly. The entire proof box, (where the bread is placed to rise up,) was full, and every single cart I had was full…such was the way…that early in the morning.

However, despite the fact that I didn't give two flaming piles of dog shit about the two sluts, or their quest to suck a cock to get on television, I had started the rolls fairly quickly. I simply didn't have room for their shit…not yet, but it was set up…what else could I really do? The two desperate cunts simply didn't understand the workings of a bakery, that things took time. They really believed they could just walk up, demand 100 freshly made rolls, then stroll away with them…all for free mind you.

"No," I replied, honest, busy with a rack of bread, finding the question…insane.

The two sluts rolled their eyes…then walked away, their little spandex, G-string asses shaking and jiggling as they walked…shaking their money makers.

5 minutes later...

(You can't make this shit up...it was 5 minutes later when they came back.)

"Are they ready yet?" Tiffany barked, hands on her hips, angry, Christine by her side, both trying to act important...despite being nobodies.

The pans were still on the table. I had just finished preparing the same rack I was working on when they first came up...I hadn't had a chance to even consider it. Seriously...it had been 5 minutes.

"No," I replied, now a little annoyed, having far more important things to do.

"We asked for them an hour ago!" Christine snapped.

While Tiffany was a slut, Christine was a slut beyond sluts. She had actually been caught, pants down, tits on the desk, ass up, getting pumped by her previous store manager before being sent to my store...all for promotion, a chance for one. Much like the Catholic church though, or the activities that take place at a Trump owned establishment, papers were signed, people were moved, and the whole thing was brushed aside. The only reason we knew about it at my store was due to the fact that she bragged openly about it...all the time. There was a certain ranking system among promotion whores and having had a store manager in your pussy...well, that was a star on your uniform, a badge of honor.

"It's been 15 minutes," I laughed, continuing what I was doing.

Again, the two cock hunting bimbos walked away.

A couple minutes later, I managed to get the rolls on a cart...and they were in the proof box, still frozen solid...not at all the best way to do things...a hurry job as is.

As soon as the rolls were in the proof box, still a good 30 minutes from being ready for the oven...at least, the two half-wits returned, but they weren't alone this time. Bryce Bobinson, playing the role of store manager, as Joe, our previous pervert overlord, had finally been sent away after countless complaints, most of the sexual nature, not that Publix would ever admit that, was with the twits with tits, looking angry, his squinty eyes and freakishly bushy eyebrows in full rage mode. The man looked like an idiot, as usual, always lost and confused, completely full of shit, just doing as the sluts demanded of him in hopes of a little sucky suck in return...trained in the arts of crooked management by Joe and years of Publix training.

"Where are those rolls!!?" Bryce barked, trying to show his ass, being a tough guy for the two walking G-strings. "They've been asking for them for over an hour!"

"It's been 20 minutes," I replied. "I just put them in the proof box like a minute ago."

"Get the rolls in the oven!" Bryce barked, then made some bizarre hand gesture, signaling to my big tittied department manager, Sarah, who had just walked in and had no idea what was happening, to come out and speak to him…alone, obviously about me, which she did.

*My store had a freakish delight, Joe and Bryce, of talking about its employees, the ones it didn't like, right in front of their faces, like they were dogs.

Sarah, while at least having more of a clue to the inner workings of a bakery than Bryce and the two twits did, not to mention my useless asst manager, who was doing nothing but hiding during Bryce's ignorant outburst, was still a product of Publix perversion. She had enormous tits, beautiful and milky white, and knew how to use them. I say they were milky white because she knew when, where, and to who to allow one to slip out…for a complete view. She tended to wear a strap, not a bra, a strap, that lifted her tits up, nearly to her chin, under her see-through white bakery shirt. They were nice…not gonna lie, but they were her tools, what ultimately got her promoted…and she knew it.

Angry, I pulled the pans of rolls, still frozen, out of the proof box…and into the oven, damn near having to put them in sideways on a rack because there was no room.

 Bryce was a clueless buffoon…he really was, a limp dick pervert, lost in every moment, hiding behind a name tag that said he was someone important.

(I have never wished a man dead, but I have read some obituaries with great pleasure. -Clarence Darrow.)

 Twelve minutes later, hard as rocks, about the size of quarters, the rolls came out of the oven. Disgusted, I then handed the rolls to a woman that processed the department's bread…washing my hands of the whole ridiculous thing. Once they were packaged, the two idiot girls took the box they were in, gave me filthy looks, then stormed away with them, off to suck as many cocks as they could to get on television.

 A few minutes later, Sarah was called upstairs…and then I was. Bryce the fool needed to have a word with us.

Chapter 2.

The cave wasn't very big, probably the size of most people's bedroom. It was large enough to sit comfortably in, and plenty big enough, and open enough, to have a small fire in. Todd had come here before with guys, smoking weed, drinking beers, as guys will do, talking about girls and their failings to acquire one. It was far rarer to get a girl to the cave though, especially at night, even she did trust you, or had let you spread her legs before.

It was just Todd this time, all alone, feeding his small fire twigs.

He had been there a while…thinking and thinking.

As the sun went down, Todd added a couple larger pieces of wood to the fire. He wasn't afraid of the night, of being alone in the cave, but there were bears in these woods, and panthers…or so he was always told, having never seen one of either in these woods. Hell, the only animal he had ever seen in these woods were squirrels, birds, racoons, and the occasional opossum. Whatever had once lived in these woods, anything larger, had long ago been hunted to local extinction by gun freak right-wing rednecks. No, the fire was something else…something spiritual, a tool, like a hammer to a carpenter.

The hours went by, well into the night, a light rain began to fall, a chill filled the air. Todd just kept nursing the fire, adding twig after twig, leaf after leaf.

Everything was perfect.

And then…

"Back again?" A voice, scratchy, gargled, suddenly said.

Todd took a deep breath…he knew who the voice belonged to, but he dared not look at it, the one the voice belonged to…not yet anyway. "It's me again," he replied, nodding his head, dropping a handful of twigs to the fire. "You came quick this time. You must have a lot to say."

The cave filled with laughter. "Do I?" The voice asked, then a figured appeared on the other side of the fire. It was a demon, taking the form of one of Todd's friends, Mike, who had died only a few days earlier. It, the demon, obviously meant business…this was far more aggressive than usual.

Todd still didn't look at the demon, keeping his eyes on the fire, watching every flame burst into life…then fade away. "Where would you like to start?" he eventually asked.

Again, the demon laughed. "I guess that's up to you. How about…from the beginning?"

The demon changed form, now appearing as Todd's deceased grandmother, having died when he was a junior in high school.

Todd couldn't help but look this time. He hadn't seen his grandmother in so long, nearly 20 years, so long in fact that the image of her now…was hard to remember. Of course, this was not his grandmother, it was a demon, trying to get inside his head, its red eyes trying to pierce his soul…as they had before.

The demon knew what buttons to push.

"You don't even remember her, do you?" The demon growled, squatting down by the fire, putting a hand into the flames.

Todd looked away from the demon. "That's not fair," he then said, shaking his head, "I was only a kid."

"17," the demon replied. "You were 17…is that a kid?"

Todd shook his head again. "I barely even…I don't even remember it, where I even was."

"Liar!" The demon snapped. "You know where you were."

"School," Todd finally admitted. "I was in school."

The demon pulled its hand out of the fire, the skin falling away from it, burn, the bone and muscles still in flames. "Your mother told you…the day before, that she wouldn't be around much longer…that she was dying. What did she ask you…that morning, before school?"

Todd didn't have to think about it…he had dwelled on it, what his mother had asked him that morning…every day since. "She asked me if I wanted to go see her…one last time."

"And what did you say?"

Todd took a deep breath, then looked at the demon. "No…I said no."

The demon laughed.

Todd looked back into the flames. "I was just a kid."

The demon blew the fire out on its hand, then its eyes turned black, it began to rot. "She died the next day," it then said, looking down at Todd, slowly decomposing, turning into bone. "You didn't feel…anything."

Todd tossed a stick in the fire…not responding.

The demon vanished…leaving Todd alone with his thoughts.

Todd knew it wasn't over yet…the demon would return.

That's why he had come to the cave.

It was going to be a long night.

---}

Todd added a few more sticks to the fire, then got up and stretched himself out a bit, taking a quick look at the rain coming down outside. Eventually though, knowing that he had much more to deal with…between he and the demon, he returned to the fire and sat back down beside it.

The demon had started strong, far more aggressive than usual. The memory of his grandmother was painful, surprisingly so. He hadn't lied though, he was young when she had died, at least in the grand scheme of things…but not that young. He had managed to bury the memory of it, her death, his failure to visit her on her death bed, with a mountain of youthful memories, pointless all, a defense mechanism he had mastered to avoid the truth…that he had been a coward that day.

 The demon had used this tactic against him before though, many times actually. He, the demon, knew it was a wound that ran deep, that it was not something he ever spoke of, not to anyone. However, this memory alone would not be enough to break Todd, and the demon knew this as well…but it was a good start, a shot to the heart.

 "How about the girls you loved?" A voice suddenly asked.

The demon had returned…and in a new form.

Todd looked at the demon, actually managing to laugh a little at what he saw. The demon had taken the form of a girl, a thin blonde that he had absolutely adored throughout his school years…Wendy White. "Are you really going there?" He asked the demon, barely recognizing the girl it was pretending to be, having not seen her for nearly as long as his deceased grandmother. "Are you going to talk about my failures with women now?"

The demon slanted its head, nearly putting its cheek on its shoulder, its black eyes fixed on Todd. "Do you want to?" It then asked. "There's so much to talk about. I'm not sure we would have the time."

The demon turned into another girl, a brunette beauty Todd had loved, not that the love was shared…at all, named Jennifer Rohback…but it only stayed there, in that form, long enough for Todd to see her, the girl. A moment later, the demon was another girl, a thin brunette, another girl Todd had fancied, Heather Tuten, then immediately changing into another, Mellisa Moore…then it, the demon, began to rapidly change from one to another, adding a few more girls as it did so, Jessica, Sarah, Mandy…on and on.

Todd watched the demon, remembering the girls, a look back on all of his failed romances, most having never even existed, just meaningless crushes he had had over the years, most of them girls that he was simply too terrified to speak to. None of them, the girls…had ever wanted him…for anything, certainly not a boyfriend…a lover.

"You know I'm above this," Todd finally said, looking back into the fire. "All ugly men deal with a long history of rejection."

The demon returned to the form of Wendy…now nude, which was a twist to the game, but nothing new. "Is this where the dream started?" It then asked, squatting down, touching its breasts…teasing.

This was something new.

"What dream?" Todd asked, a bit taken back now.

The demon laughed. "The dream that any woman would love you.

The words hit Todd hard. The demon had formulated a new attack plan…this was not normal…it was far more cruel than usual. "What exactly do you want me to say?" He asked, a bit timid, not sure where this was going…other than a new path. "Do you want me to admit that I'm not exactly a ladies' man?"

"I want you to admit to me…that no woman…has ever loved you," the demon replied, now touching other parts of itself. "I want you to admit it…to yourself…now."

Todd didn't reply, looking deep into the fire, the subject bothering him, that once again the demon knew too much…a terrible truth.

The demon changed forms…this time becoming a girl that Todd had very much loved in his youth…Carol, a beautiful blonde with long hair and large breasts. "Do you think this one loved you?" It then asked, nasty-like, hateful.

Todd looked at the demon, remembering the girl…the love lost…the love never achieved. "I don't know," he then replied, honest. "I guess…well, I guess I hoped that she had."

The demon laughed. "She never made any effort to be with you."

That made Todd angry. "That's not true!" He fired back, instantly regretting it, knowing the demon had struck a blow. "We were together…once," he then said, calming himself, putting up all his defenses again.

The demon smiled. "You spilled your seed inside her in 3 minutes," it then laughed. "Is that the way women…want it…was she…impressed?"

Todd didn't reply…trying not to remember the brief love-making session the two had shared…an embarrassment then…and now. She, Carol, had crawled through his window that night…and they had indeed made love…but Todd, beyond excited, had fired off inside her minutes after entering her…and that was that, they never made love again, in fact, Carol moved away not long after.

"You weren't even sure it actually happened," the demon then laughed.

The demon wasn't lying. Todd fell asleep after cumming inside Carol…and he awoke, she was gone. For a long time, he wasn't even sure it had really happened, not until Carol's cousin, Rosy, spoke of it years later, saying Carol had come back home, worried, upset that she might get pregnant.

She hadn't…which in its own way, however wrong it may have been, was another failure of Todd's. If he had impregnated her…who knows, maybe his life would have been very different…maybe not.

"You never saw her again…did you?" The demon asked. "She never made any attempt to see you after that…did she?"

"No," Todd replied. "She moved away…then I moved away."

"And…what happened to her?" The demon asked…knowing, just wanting to hear.

"I don't know," Todd lied.

"Liar!" The demon snapped. "You know damn well what happened to her."

Todd didn't say anything.

"She married some filthy redneck and had 4 kids," the demon laughed. "So, the girl was obviously a healthy female, capable of being bred…just not by you."

"I had heard something like that," Todd admitted, having heard that she, Carol, had married some loser and had several children.

"Still think she loved you?"

Todd shrugged his shoulders. "I don't know," he then replied.

The demon laughed…then vanished.

A chill filled the air.

Todd had lost that round.

---}

Todd walked to the cave entrance, then out, into the rain. He wasn't leaving, he needed to pee. As he did so, a crow, a big crow, called out, up high in a tree beside the cave, looking down at him as he peed.

“What?” Todd asked, looking up at the crow.

The crow looked right at Todd, its eyes glowing in the dark, rather sinister looking...then it let out a loud caw, as if replying.

Todd laughed. “Is that right?”

The crow cawed again.

“Well, I guess I won’t argue with you about that.”

Todd zipped up his pants, then turned to enter the cave again.

Just then though…there was a sound.

Todd turned around.

Coming at him was a dog, a wiener dog…one he knew very well.

"Chubs," Todd said, shocked, eyes wide.

The dog had died the previous year…his idiot friend had killed it, supposedly on accident…supposedly.

Todd knew what was happening now, looking back up at the crow. "Come on," he said, speaking to the crow, which was not a crow, he knew that now, "that's outside the lines…that's too new. I haven't even had a chance to deal with that yet."

The crow let out a loud caw, rather like a laugh, then vanished…then the dog vanished.

"I guess we will save that for later," a voice, back inside the cave, said.

Todd walked back into the cave. The demon had returned, sitting beside the fire, its feet in the flames.

It had taken a new form…one Todd knew instantly…not that he could ever forget her.

Gwen Goldsmith…the first to be the last.

The demon watched Todd walk up to the fire, not saying a word…it didn't have to.

"At it again, huh?" Todd said, looking at the demon, the figure it was in. "You'll have to do better than that. I've had years to work out my demons with that one."

Todd sat down across from the demon, the fire between them.

The demon laughed, knowing better…that there was a mountain of pain that came with this girl. "Have you now?"

"Many times over," Todd replied, trying to sound confident, wanting nothing to do with this line of attack.

The demon knew though…it had twisted this knife before.

"You think she loved you?" The demon asked, holding its left foot up from the flames, watching it burn, the flesh melt off.

"At one point," Todd replied, but then shook the words away. "I don't know. All I do know is she had problems."

The demon lowered its foot back into the flames...looking at Todd, perhaps thinking about its next move.

"Yes, she did have problems," the demon finally said, after a brief silence. "Do you remember when she told you about her grandfather dying? Do you remember what she said about being too fat to help, too lazy...that she blamed herself? Do you remember that, when she broke down in tears over it?"

Todd scrunched his face, remembering it, that moment, all too well. "She told me a lot of stories," he then replied. "Lots and lots of stories...most of which were complete bullshit."

"What about when her uncle sexually abused her?" The demon quickly asked, pushing forward with its attack. "Was that bullshit?"

"You mean the uncle that she ran off to live with the first time she left?" Todd snapped, angry. "Just another fucking lie she told me."

The demon began to laugh.

"What?" Todd asked, calming down, angry now that he had allowed the demon to touch a nerve…a sensitive one, even after all the years.

"You didn't always think it was a lie," the demon eventually said, waiting for Todd to calm down. "Remember the truck?"

Todd was instantly angry again…or maybe embarrassed…ashamed. "Of course," he finally said, sinking into himself, remembering that night like it was yesterday…every aspect of it. "The dumbest thing I ever did…all for her…because of her lies."

"You stole that truck so you could go be with her…to protect her from that uncle. You obviously believed it then. You were worried about her…you loved her."

"She fucking left me to go be up there…with him!" Todd nearly shouted. "She could have stayed…she gave up on us."

"And when she came back the next year?

"She was with some loser," Todd said, trying to calm down, the memories of it all hitting him hard. "She left me and was fucking some loser in a matter of days…I never meant shit."

The demon laughed.

It had won that round easily.

--}

The demon shifted around a little, finally pulling its feet, now just blackened bone, out of the fire. (They immediately returned to normal though, after a couple seconds.) "She left that guy, the loser, as you call him, almost immediately after she returned though…for you, right? You two were together again?"

"Yeah," Todd admitted, picking up a stick, poking the fire with it.

"And, how did that go?"

Todd laughed at that. "She left me again…for some fat fucking slob."

The demon looked at Todd, not saying a word…for several moments.

"What?" Todd finally asked, uncomfortable with the silence.

"Why did she leave?" The demon finally asked. "I think there is something more to this than you care to admit…not even to yourself."

Todd nearly barked something back, the same excuse he had used over the years, the one he gave to the world…but then, from out of nowhere, from deep inside his buried memories…a thought crossed his mind, one he had not considered in many years. "That fucking nerd," he mumbled, remembering a face behind thick glasses.

"What nerd?"

"KC."

The demon turned into a young man, a boy really. This boy had a bend to his back, a long nose, and half-inch thick glasses on his face…he looked every part a nerd. "You were jealous of this?" The demon laughed. "You were jealous of this nerd?"

Todd didn't answer, the image of the boy, even now, bringing back strong memories…anger.

The demon could feel Todd's anger. "You drove her away…because of this?"

That night, when Gwen left him for the second time, played out in Todd's mind.

He hadn't thought about it in a very long time. The demon hadn't gone this route in a while...years...but it was still there, the pain.

The demon laughed.

Todd looked at the demon, angry.

The demon suddenly turned into a fat man...a really fat man, disgusting looking, in tiny shorts and a shirt much too small for him. "You drove her into the arms of this...thing?" The demon seemed to look at itself, disgusted by what it was seeing, the fat under its arms, its belly.

"I didn't make her fuck that fat bastard," Todd replied, suddenly filled with a very old anger, one that ran very deep. "She ran to him...to..."

Todd stopped himself...but it was too late.

"To what?" The demon asked...knowing.

"To make me jealous," Todd replied, remembering.

"She went there...to see you, didn't she?"

Todd remembered the day after their fight, when Gwen showed up at the alley, dressed real nice…obviously there to see him.

"What did you do?" The demon asked.

Todd felt a sting of shame. "I made fun of her," he admitted. "I was with a friend…and I guess I…"

"Had to look cool?"

Todd didn't reply, looking into the fire, remembering…remembering her running out the door…coming back later…with him, the fat man…Andy. He had driven her straight to him.

The demon stood up, feeling something, something it hadn't felt in a long time…a weakness. It was winning this battle.

The demon vanished.

Todd sat beside the fire, soaked in regret.

--}

The demon returned a few minutes later, sitting across the fire, saying nothing. It had broken through, taking down years' worth of mental barriers that Todd had put up. Gwen had broken his heart…multiple times, and deep down, at least in some way, he had been to blame for her leaving him. He had never admitted this though, and even know, with all his defenses down, his mind franticly worked to reconstruct the barriers, sending him a barrage of half-truths and straight out lies, all constructed within itself to shield away the pain…no matter how many years went by.

"Build those walls high," the demon finally said.

Todd looked at the demon, which was again in the form of Gwen, now wearing the John Elway jersey that Todd had bought for her, meant to match the one he had…the one she wore once…the day she left him the first time.

"But you guys were not done yet…were you?" The Demon asked.

"No," Todd replied.

"She came back…a third time?"

"Yes."

The demon laughed. "And…how did that go?"

"She fucking cheated on me!" Todd snapped, surprising even himself a bit that the anger came so quick. "She fucked some married guy, some loser who thought he was important because he was in the air force."

Todd felt that he was in the right this time, confident that she, Gwen, was the one at fault…this time.

The demon grinned. "You're right…she did cheat," it replied, seemingly giving in on that point, that she was at fault…at least in some way, "but what drove her away that time? Surely it wasn't simply a thirst for a married man's cock."

"We were broke," Todd replied, remembering, allowing them, the memories, to come to him, at least the ones he allowed to come to him, "and she wanted to play, to go everywhere, spend money we didn't have…" Suddenly a thought came to Todd's mind, a memory, a truth, one he hadn't thought of in a great while.

The demon laughed.

"I don't want to talk about that," Todd quickly said, shutting the door on the demon, pushing the thought out of his mind, burying it.

"If you insist," the demon replied, "but blocking me out…"

"I said no," Todd quickly said, looking at the demon, serious.

The demon smiled. "Alright, there are so many other things to speak of. How about we talk about…your parents? Something bad happened, just about the same time as you were getting back together with Gwen that 3rd time…didn't it?"

Todd was taken a bit off guard. "You mean…when my parents got divorced?" he asked, not sure where the demon was going now, not sure what walls to bring up.

"That's a start," the demon hissed, feeling perhaps that Todd was avoiding something…a deep buried truth. "What did your father tell you?"

Suddenly Todd had a very good sense of where the demon was going with its line of questions.

"You mean after he told me that I was a disappointment?" Todd asked, remembering when his father had said that to him one night, drunk out of his mind.

The demon laughed hard at that. "No," it finally replied, then gave Todd a serious look. "Would you like to talk about that?"

"No."

The demon laughed again.

Suddenly Todd remembered something. "You want to talk about the time my father told me he was going to leave the minute I turned 18?"

The demon nodded his head, yes. "We barely got into that…during our last talk."

"What else is there to talk about?" Todd asked, poking the fire with a stick. "It seems pretty straight forward…he said he was leaving when I was 18…and he did."

"There's more to it," the demon hissed. "Your father left after…what?"

"When I was 18," Todd repeated.

"No!" The demon shouted, causing the fire to grow, making shadows move on the walls. "You are shielding me from something, something you do not want to remember!"

Covering his eyes from the suddenly much brighter fire, Todd was just about to shout something back…when a truth came to him, possibly for the first time.

"He left…right after my grandfather died," he said, the words stinging him as they came out of his mouth, the memory of that time hitting him hard."

The fire returned to normal. "very good," the demon said, now in a new form, that of an old man, sickly, frail, on death's doorstep. It was Todd's grandfather, just days before he died…or so it appeared. "Your father left, left her, left you, right after your grandfather died…didn't he?"

Todd didn't reply, lost in the image of his dead grandfather…how awful he looked, after a lifetime of being so…strong, lively.

The demon laughed. "I can hear your thoughts," it then said. "Something about…him…shitting the bed, spreading it all over the wall, all over the floor. That was the moment that your mother…gave up. She had been trying to take care of him before that…but he wouldn't let a nurse help…and she was falling apart…right in front of your eyes…then that morning…it was too much."

"Yes," Todd replied, deep in thought, remembering it, that morning, the shit all over the wall, on the floor…everywhere. He could remember it…all of it, even the smell.

"That was when you realized…he was dying," the demon said, matter of fact like…knowing.

Todd didn't reply…but the demon was right, that was when the reality of it all, that his grandfather was truly near death, sunk in for the first time.

"Where did you go…that day, after finding the shit all over the wall?"

Todd didn't remember at first…but then it came to him…along with the shame.

Suddenly the demon changed form again, becoming Gwen again. "You went to her…she was there for you…in that moment."

That comment angered Todd. "Only because I went to her!" He shot back, angry.

"Leaving your mother…all alone, all alone to deal with her dying father…and a shit covered wall."

Todd realized that the demon had tricked him, had led him to this awful truth. "Yes," he replied, ashamed. "I left her…to deal with it. I guess…well, I guess I couldn't handle it."

Suddenly, out of nowhere, Todd remembered something…something that had managed to root its way to the surface…after being buried for a very long time.

The demon exploded with laughter. Todd had just exposed a great pain to it, something new to torment him with…a brand-new weapon.

---}

The Demon sat silent for a few in minutes, back in its demon form, its hellish face stuck in a way that made it appear to be laughing, its head tilted to the right…. staring at Todd with dead eyes.

Todd did his best to ignore it…but he knew it was only a matter off time. The demon was working out its next move, setting its strategy.

"Your mother put him in the hospital after that?" The Demon finally said, coming back to life…so to speak.

"Yes," Todd admitted, knowing where the demon was going with this new line of questions, preparing himself for what it was about to do, how it was going to attack him.

"And how many times did you…go see him…at the hospital?"

Todd took a deep breath, then looked directly at the demon, perhaps trying to show strength. "Once," he then said. "I went to see him…once."

"With…"

"Gwen."

"You took her with you…to see him on his death bed…why?"

"I don't know," Todd replied, looking back into the flames, remembering, seeing his grandfather, so close to death.

"Liar!" The demon barked. "If you can't be honest with me…than who?"

Todd knew the answer…deep down, but he also knew how ugly it was…the truth of it, why had brought her with him that day.

"Well?" The demon pressured, not letting it go.

"So…so I wouldn't have to stay long," Todd admitted, ashamed, disgusted by it, mad at himself, the memories it let break free…what a pathetic person he had been that day.

The demon seemed to absorb the words Todd spoke…gaining power from them, remembering a time not so long ago when Todd would not speak them, not even to himself.

Todd was consumed by the memory of that day…he could see it with his mind's eye, like it was happening right there, all over again, all these years later. He could see his grandfather, dying, in that disgusting bed, another man a few feet away in another bed…also dying. It was a room of death.

Desperate, Todd tried to throw up all his defensive shields, to choke the memory back down…as deep as it could go.

"What did he say?" The demon suddenly asked, refusing to stop, driving the nail in even deeper, not letting Todd build the wall around the memory again.

Todd hesitated for a couple seconds, remembering, not liking the memory at all. "He said…you don't have to stay," he finally replied, the words stinging.

"You don't have to stay," the demon repeated. "So, your plan worked?"

"I guess so," Todd replied, disgusted with himself.

The demon smiled. "He died that night?"

"Yes," Todd replied.

"Your mother had to deal with that too…no doubt with lots of help from you?" The demon asked, sarcastic, digging its claws in deeper.

"No," Todd replied, giving the demon a look of aggravation, knowing it was trying to drive the fact, the hurt, in as deep as it could now.

"No?" The demon asked, not at all affected by Todd's look of disapproval. "Where did you go?"

"To Gwen's...again."

"To Gwen's?" The demon laughed. "So, just like when you left her after her husband, your father, left her...you left her when her father died...to go be with your girlfriend...to get yourself some pussy?"

"Yes," Todd admitted, ashamed, angry.

The demon laughed...then slowly vanished.

Todd was alone again...

Outside, the rain began to fall again...lightning flashed, and thunder rumbled inside the cave.

--}

Chapter 3.

Todd wasn't alone very long…not this time. The demon meant business this night…

"Tell me," the demon said, suddenly appearing in the cave again, walking towards Todd, stepping right through the fire to stand in front of him…then it squatted down, looking him in the eyes, "how did your mother handle it all…her husband leaving, her father dying…you running off with your precious Gwen?"

Todd hesitated. The demon was using the memory he had managed to pull up from Todd's memory a few minutes earlier. This was something new…and that gave it, the demon, the advantage. "Not well," he admitted, cautious, not entirely sure what to conceal…how much the demon already knew.

"That night…in your room," the demon began, rather slowly, perhaps putting things together, its attack, together as it went. "Your mother knocked on your bedroom door…what did she say that night?"

Now Todd understood where the demon was going with all this. In his head, an image appeared, one he had blocked out for…ages…years and years. It was a terrible memory, one that bothered him as much now, in the cave, as it did that night. "She offered me…my grandfather's…underwear," he replied, remembering his mother, the crazed look on his mother's face that night, like nothing he had ever seen before. "She said when wore it…his other clothes, his shirts, that she could feel him…as if he were alive somehow."

The demon stood up, then walked back through the fire, sitting down on the other side of it, across from Todd again, looking at him intently…it could feel something, something new, a fresh pain. "It scared you…didn't it?" It then asked.

Todd hesitated for a moment. The image of his mother, the look on her face, the way she was touching herself, trying to hand him his dead grandfather's underwear…it was heavy on his mind…crushing everything else. "Yes," he eventually replied, honest, not even realizing he had spoken, not till the word was out of his mouth, rather like the truth wanted out…after years and years.

"You told her…no?"

"Of course, I fucking did!" Todd replied, angry, slamming the door shut on the image, the memory.

"Of course, you did," the demon replied, letting the memory fade a bit, perhaps realizing it had angered Todd more than it had intended…but only for a moment. "She was slipping…wasn't she?"

Todd didn't reply, far too busy pushing the memory back, deep down, rapidly constructing new mental blocks, natural defenses against the awful memory.

"What happened next?" The demon pressured, once Todd had calmed down a bit, not allowing him to sink into himself too far.

Todd wasn't sure if the demon knew more, or more likely, that it did, possibly a lot more, and was trying to pull more out while it had him on his heels a bit. "What do you want to know?" he asked, cautious, testing the waters, not wanting to get swept away.

"I want to know…about the gun."

(*Shit*,) Todd thought, very much aware now that the demon knew more, a lot more…maybe too much. "You want to know about the night that I came home to find her writing her will?"

"More!" The demon barked, causing the fire to grow for a moment. "I want to know about the gun! Don't block it out!"

Todd hadn't thought about that night in a very long time. For better or worse, he had managed to push the memory deep down…but then he did remember it, rather all at once…but then something else slipped out…broke free.

The demon laughed…having just received something new…more ammunition. "The inner anguish never ends with you," it then said, shaking its head at Todd. "How much is there…down in the depths?"

"You should know," Todd replied, looking into the flames now.

"Tell me...about that night?" The demon pressed, its voice deeper now...more serious.

Todd hesitated, reliving the night in his mind, then he looked at the demon, into its evil eyes. "Well," he began, "I came home to find my mother...writing her will...with a gun on the table."

"What did she say?"

Again, Todd hesitated. Not so much due to the fact it was so long ago, that it was hard to remember, but rather due to the fact that it, what his mother said to him, still bothered him...and had caused him problems years later. "She told me...that she wanted me and my brother to...fight over everything...and to give him nothing."

The demon laughed at that. "That doesn't sound very...loving. What did you do after that?"

"I called the police."

"The police?" The demon laughed. "What happened then?"

"They…when they arrived, saw the gun…and…shoved her against the wall."

"Why?"

Todd didn't like the next part. He had never really lingered on the moment very long…knowing the awful truth of it. "When she saw them…the cops, she suddenly became…very sober…very aware of herself," he replied, remembering it all, hearing the dogs barking in his mind, as if it were all happening right now, seeing it all in his head.

"Why did they shove her against the wall then, if she was suddenly completely sober?"

"When she stood up, one of the cops saw…" Todd began, but then something else slipped out, a buried memory.

The demon took the memory in, a look of pure pleasure on its hideous face. "Delicious," it said, devouring the memory…new material to use.

"The cops…the cop, saw an old rifle…when she stood up, and thought she was reaching for it," Todd finally finished, ignoring the demon, its delight in the moment.

"She wasn't?"

"Of course not," Todd snapped.

The demon laughed at Todd's aggravation...but it didn't stop him. "You say she went back to normal...once the cops arrived?"

"Yes."

"Well, if that's true...doesn't that mean...it was all..."

"For attention," Todd said, cutting the demon off.

 The demon nodded his head, yes. "So, it was...a cry for help...from the son who kept running away when she needed him?"

Todd didn't reply to that...he didn't need to...the demon was right.

"So, where did she end up?"

"The funny farm," Todd replied.

The demon laughed. "So, your mother made a desperate cry for help…after her husband left her…after her father died, from the son who refused to help her…and you sent her…to the loony bin?"

"Yes…"

The demon laughed.

---}

Todd sat alone for several minutes, just feeding the fire stick after stick. He knew the demon wasn't gone, but the delay…was not normal. It had won every round thus far, and opened new doors, resurfaced memories that had been buried for many years. It was not like it at all to give him this much time to recover…not at all.

It was up to something.

"Tell me about…the chickens," a voice suddenly said.

Startled, Todd turned around.

Standing in the corner of the cave, in the shadows, was the demon.

"The chickens?" Todd asked, confused, adjusting the way he was sitting to better see the demon, not comfortable with it being behind him...unwatched.

The demon growled, then shook its head, stepping out of the shadows now. "Why play these games?" It then asked. "We've come so far."

Todd thought for a moment, a little surprised by the request, how the demon would use it, the memory, against him. It was a completely different kind of memory, albeit just as terrible as the others, at least to him...just different.

"Well?" The demon asked, now pacing a bit, back and forth, in and out of the shadows.

"The racoons were killing them," Todd finally said, remembering...being cautious though, not at all sure where the demon was heading this time.

The demon smiled. "That's a start," it then said. "Now, go on."

"The chickens were the last animals we had...from when it was...a ranch," Todd explained, feeling very bad, hating the memory. "My mother...asked me to fix up the chicken coop...or the racoons would kill them."

"And…did you?"

"I tried," Todd replied, ashamed.

 The demon stopped its pacing and gazed at Todd for a moment. "You're shielding something," it then said. "What happened with the chicken coop? Did you fix it…or not?"

"Not really," Todd finally admitted, falling into himself a bit, not liking the memory. "I tried…but…I knew the racoons could get in."

"You let the racoons kill the chickens?"

Todd looked at the demon, angry. "No…I didn't want them to."

"But…they did?"

Todd lowered his head, ashamed of the memory. "Yes," he admitted. "They came back that night…and killed almost every one of them."

The demon tiled its head, looking at Todd. "This memory…bothers you," it then said, seemingly surprised by the pain it caused Todd. "Why?"

Todd took a moment, then he looked at the demon. "For a couple reasons."

"Go on."

Todd managed a laugh, albeit a painful one.

"What?" The demon asked, finally walking up to the fire, sitting down across from Todd again.

Todd looked at the demon. "I know this will sound…crazy," he then began, "but I think they knew…that I was their only hope."

Todd could see them, the chickens, their faces, the look of terror on them, knowing what the night brought...death...the racoons.

"But you still let them die?" The demon asked.

"I didn't want them to!" Todd quickly replied, honest.

"But they did...why?"

Todd took a deep breath, then looked into the flames. "I didn't put any real effort into it...fixing the coop."

"So, you were...lazy?"

"Yes."

"Just like...your father?"

The demon's words hit Todd hard. "Yes," he admitted.

The demon laughed.

"But...what made it even worse," Todd continued, surprising the demon, causing it to stop laughing, "was that it...really ended...everything."

"How?"

Todd poked at the fire with a stick, then looked at the demon. "When I was a kid...when we first moved there...to our little ranch, we had chickens, cows, pigs, a goat, even a few geese, but after that night...they were all gone...mostly. It just felt like...the end of something, like a piece of my youth...was gone...forever."

The demon didn't have to say anything...it was basking in the pain...the pain that a few dead chickens had brought.

--}

Chapter 4.

The demon sat silent for several minutes. As Todd worked through the memories it, the demon, had stirred up, dealing with them however he could, it was measuring its next assault. Finally though, just when it seemed Todd might have come to some bit of peace with it all, the demon launched itself into its next attack…back in the form of Gwen.

"You and Gwen still found each other again?" The demon asked, ending its silence.

Caught a little off-guard, a memory slipped out of Todd's mind. He quickly tried to bury it, this memory…but it was too late.

The demon caught it.

"A car?" The demon asked, excited, feeling this memory it had captured was something new. "A pretty, little red car? Tell me about it…what it meant to you."

Todd was mad at himself for allowing the memory to escape just then. It was often on his mind though, escaping more often than he wished. It was one of the dumbest things he had ever done…and it haunted him still…like a curse.

"It was a 96 Camaro," Todd explained, seeing the car in his mind, remembering how it sounded, how it smelled, how much he loved to drive it.

The demon laughed, surprised by the emotions it was feeling, how much the subject, the car, bothered Todd. "Tell me about it," it said, running its right hand through the flames…Gwen's right hand, watching the flesh turn black and burn away.

"My grandfather bought it for me," Todd explained.

"Really?" The demon asked, seemingly surprised by the statement.

"Yes, when I was 18," Todd continued, then, for a brief moment, allowed another memory to slip free.

The demon caught the escaped memory, absorbing it.

"It wasn't your.... first car though?" The demon asked, using the escaped memory right away, finding it too interesting, and relevant, to let slide by.

"No," Todd replied, shaking his head, no. "My first car was actually an old Mercury."

The demon hesitated for a moment, taking in Todd's feelings. "You hated that car...and yet...loved it at the same time?" It eventually asked.

Todd nodded his head, yes, not even attempting to argue with the demon.

"What happened?" The demon asked. "Why were you so torn about the car…even now?"

Todd managed a little laugh.

"What?" The demon asked.

"My first car was supposed to be a red Fiero," Todd explained. "From the time I started to dream of driving, I always knew my first car would be a Fiero…red and beautiful…there was never any doubt, that was my car. I loved it before I ever drove it."

"You never got it?"

Todd shook his head, yes. "Oh, I got it," he replied. "My car was there, at the house, forever, from the time that I was 13...I saw it every day."

"What happened?"

"About a year before my 18th birthday, I came home from school to find that my father had...cut the car in half," Todd explained.

"What?" The demon laughed. "Why?"

Todd shrugged his shoulders. "Not only did he cut the car in half...for whatever reason, but he had also torn it to pieces, the wires, interior, the doors, motor...everything. It was spread out across the garage, the barn...everywhere."

"I take it he...never put it back together again?"

Todd rolled his eyes at that question, as if it were ridiculous to even ask. "hell no," he then said. "I knew the instant I saw it like that, all torn up, that he was never going to put it back together again."

"And you have no idea why he did it?"

"No, not really."

"Not really?" The demon asked, pushing for something more.

Todd shook his head, annoyed with himself for believing he could say something like that to the demon and expect it to simply slide by. "I don't know," he began, "maybe...I just...eventually came to believe that he did it on purpose."

"Why would he do that?"

"So he wouldn't have to deal with it," Todd replied, remembering what a tremendous mess the car was once his father was done destroying it.

"Don't you think that's a little extreme?" The demon asked, finally removing its hand from the fire, now looking directly at Todd. "I mean, ripping the car apart must have been a hell of a job.... just to do it for nothing."

Todd shook his head, no. "He had over 5 years to do it...to fix whatever was wrong with the car," he then said, remembering, "and never once said anything about needing to cut it in half."

"So…you were disappointed…in the car…and him?"

"Yes," Todd replied, then accidentally allowed another memory to slip free.

The demon grabbed it.

"A race car?" The demon asked, using the escaped memory right away. "That was another time that he…disappointed you?"

Todd didn't reply, angry that he had allowed that memory to escape.

The demon laughed, knowing it had something good…something new.

"Tell me about the…racecar," the demon said.

"My father didn't want to race anymore," Todd quickly said, perhaps hoping he could end the discussion with a short, rather pointless answer…but he knew it went deeper than that…and if he knew it, so did the demon.

"Come on," the demon said, as Todd suspected it would. "It means more than that. If it didn't, you wouldn't have it buried so deep. Now, tell me, why didn't he want to race anymore?"

Todd took a deep breath. "I think it scared him," he then replied.

"Can you blame him for that?" The demon asked, rather surprisingly, at least to Todd. "Maybe it did…maybe it didn't. It's a dangerous sport, many people have died doing it."

Todd shrugged his shoulders, neither agreeing nor disagreeing.

"Now, tell me what happened after he quit," the demon pressed.

"He told me to drive it," Todd admitted.

"Wow, that sounds exciting. Were you excited?"

"It was all I had been dreaming about, ever sense I first watched my first race," Todd replied, though his voice was sad, pathetic. "I even had my own suit…and my own helmet."

"But…something happened, didn't it?"

"It suddenly dawned on me that I didn't even know how to drive," Todd replied, honest…somewhat.

The demon laughed. "So, you dreamed of driving a racecar…but you didn't even know how to drive? Or, is that just what you told yourself…at that moment?"

"I had driven Go-karts, 3-wheelers, and a lot of other things," Todd admitted, "but I had never driven a car…not once…ever."

So, you chickened out?"

Todd looked at the demon, angry, not liking the way that sounded, but then he just looked back into the flames of the fire…not saying a word.

The demon laughed. "But you gave your dad grief…when he…as you saw it…chickened out?"

Todd didn't reply.

"There's more to this though…what else happened?"

Todd looked into the fire, then at the demon. "The next week…my dad went back to the races…without me."

"He went without you?"

Todd nodded his head, yes. "Yes…with the car."

"With the car?" The demon asked, seemingly surprised. "So, he didn't chicken out?"

Todd shrugged his shoulders. "I don't know," he then said. "The story he told me sounded…I don't know…hard to believe."

"How so?"

"He told me that he was out there passing cars left and right," Todd explained. "He said the car ran so good that the track officials came over to inspect the car."

"Well, that sounds good," the demon replied. "I take it that you didn't believe him though?"

Todd shook his head, no. "It was all a lie."

"How do you know? After all, you weren't there."

Todd hesitated. "I just know," he eventually replied.

"Did you two ever go to the races again?"

"Just once," Todd replied, remembering.

"And, what happened then?"

"He intentionally missed the race."

"How do you know he missed the race on purpose?"

"I could see it on his face…that he was scared," Todd replied, remembering.

"What happened after that…after he missed the race?"

"We went to watch the races…and he looked at me with this strange look of shame…and asked me…if I wanted to leave," Todd explained.

"What did you say?"

"Yes," Todd replied, remembering how disappointed he was. "It was the last time we ever went to the races together. He never touched the racecar again. I'm not even sure what happened to it…in a few weeks…it was just gone."

The demon laughed. "So, another dream…destroyed?"

"Yes."

--}

"Let's go back a little," the demon said, not letting Todd off the hook, keeping the pressure on him. "There was something else though…happening around this time. Something about your mother…and a friend?"

Todd was a little caught off-guard, not at all sure what the demon was talking about. "Huh?"

"After your mother was sent to the funny farm," the demon explained, "she met a…friend?"

"Oh," Todd replied, remembering, "yeah, she met some fat woman in there."

"Inside the funny farm?"

"Yes," Todd admitted, remembering the woman, "when my mom got out, they would call each other…have lunch together."

"Sounds surprisingly…normal."

"It was," Todd admitted. "My mother never made friends. She never went out…aside from the store."

"What happened?"

"They hung out a few times," Todd explained. "I'm not real sure what they did…other than have lunch, but it was nice to see my mother have a life for a while."

"But it ended?"

"Yeah," Todd replied. "My mother stopped answering the phone. When I asked her why…why she didn't want to talk to the woman anymore, she told me that she was too fat, and that all they ever did was eat."

Just then, a thought escaped Todd's mind.

The demon gathered the escaped memory up in an instant.

"Your mother was sickly thin," the demon said, using the thought it had just gathered

"No, not yet," Todd replied, "but she was starting to get skinny. Later on though…it got real bad."

"Thin…like a skeleton?" The demon asked, knowing.

Todd thought about things, his mother, when she was at her worst…her thinnest. As he did this…the demon consumed it all…Todd's memories.

"She was an alcoholic too?" The demon eventually asked.

Todd actually laughed at that…but then a memory escaped, then another…and another.

The demon laughed, taking it all in, all the added ammunition, things they had never spoken of.

"I guess you could say that," Todd finally answered, ignoring the demon's laughter. His mother's drinking was an old topic though, one they had spoken of several times before.

"You once told me…that you didn't know she was an alcoholic?" The demon asked.

"How could that be?"

"The alcohol was always there," Todd explained. "There was always beer in the living room, cases of it, right by the garage door, and vodka on the kitchen counter…always."

"Tell me…about the cans," the demon said, using one of the escaped memories that Todd had just given away.

Todd hadn't thought about the cans in years. It had been such an innocent thing back then…in his ignorant youth. Now, looking back on it, it was a terrible thing though. "Beside the pig pens, there was a fenced off area, about six feet wide…maybe a little more…a big circle, taller than me."

"What was in it?"

"Beer cans," Todd replied. "My dad's beer cans, hundreds of them…thousands, taller than me, way over my head at times."

"They weren't all his though?" The demon asked, obviously insinuating something…something it already knew.

"No, there were a few soda cans in there too," Todd replied, playing dumb.

The demon gave Todd a sideways look. "That's not what I meant, stupid," it then said. "Not all of the beer cans were from your father…were they?"

Todd shook his head, no, honest. "No, about half of them, maybe a quarter of them, were my grandfather's. He drank pretty heavy back then too, but his beer was different…more expensive…the good stuff."

"So, your father drank…your mother drank…your grandfather drank…and…"

"My brother drinks," Todd said, knowing where the demon was going…as it had been down this road before…in one way or another.

"A family of alcoholics."

"Not anymore," Todd replied, far more defiant than he had been about anything so far.

The demon seemed to flicker for a moment…but then became solid again. "But…you have tasted the sickness before…correct?"

"Yes," Todd replied, honest.

"Alone?"

"Never," Todd declared, rather proudly. "I never drink alone."

The demon smiled.

Todd suddenly realized that the demon was building something...a new attack.

"But...you drink with your friends?"

Todd gave the demon a serious look. "We're not going to talk about that," he then declared.

The demon shook its head, then let out a disappointed chuckle. "Eventually you're going to talk to me about them."

"Eventually," Todd admitted, "but not this night."

---}

Chapter 5.

The demon paced back and forth, acting agitated. There were things that Todd was not prepared to talk about, not even to him. He would open a door, then close it immediately...and even the demon could not break through, at least not openly.

Sitting there now, Todd was silent, just feeding the fire sticks. It was raining hard now, and it was getting cold. There was water, drips, nothing heavy, running down the side of the cave's walls, which only added a certain level of gloom to the situation. On paper, the demon had the perfect environment, the perfect feeling...everything it needed to have to a breakthrough.

And it was winning the night.

But there was more...a lot more.

"You know," the demon finally said, stopping its pacing, looking at Todd again, "you came to me...I didn't come looking for you. If you're not going to talk, then why are we here? You can't be comfortable here...in this damp cave."

Todd didn't reply. In truth, the demon had already taken more than he intended for it to get that night, and he wasn't in any hurry to offer anything more.

"How about we go back to Gwen?" The demon asked, once again changing into that form, Gwen, young and pretty.

Todd laughed. "What else is there?" He asked.

The demon laughed back. "Oh come now," it then began, walking up to fire, squatting down across from Todd, "you know there is more to this story…we have barely scratched the surface."

Todd took a deep breath, then exhaled, obviously not interested in the subject.

"What about when you two managed to move in together?" The demon pressed, though it knew it was a subject they had discussed before…many times actually. "That pain never seems to diminish."

"How could there be anything more to cover with that?" Todd asked.

The demon laughed at that. "This is your show, Todd," it then said. "I wouldn't be here mentioning it if there wasn't something more to be said. Even after all these years…you're still hiding things…from me, from yourself."

"I doubt it," Todd replied, poking at the fire with a stick.

The demon gave Todd a serious look. "Is that so?"

Todd shrugged his shoulders.

The demon smiled. "Tell me about the house you guys moved into together," it then asked, rather aggressive now, aggravated with Todd. "It was a beautiful little house, right?"

This was something new, and it caught Todd by surprise. "No, it was a nasty little trailer," he replied, honest, maybe a little ashamed.

"It must have been pretty cheap to live there…if it was such a place…a nasty little trailer."

"Yeah, I guess, looking back on it, I suppose it was…at least by today's standards," Todd replied, remembering, being honest…and cautious.

"So, you guys didn't have any problems?"

Todd hesitated. He could have lied to the demon…to himself, but he was strangely curious where it, the demon, was going with its attack. "Just my stupidity," he replied, honest, allowing a hole in his defenses, giving the demon a door to walk through.

"I see," the demon replied. "So, how exactly did you…pay for the trailer?"

The trailer had come up before, in different ways, but the way that the demon was going about it this time, confused Todd, but he was sure of one thing…that the demon had a plan. "I sold my car," he replied, very cautious now.

"What car?" The demon asked, rather stupidly.

"My Camaro," Todd replied, remembering it, the car, and the terrible day that he sold it.

"You mean, the car that your grandfather…"

"Bought for me?" Todd snapped, cutting the demon off, annoyed by its attempt to play dumb. "The little red Camaro that my grandfather had bought for me."

"So, selling it was how you got the money to move into the trailer?"

"Yes," Todd replied, a well of emotions beneath the word…deep shame.

Suddenly a memory slipped free from the depths of Todd's memories.

"I knew there was more," the demon laughed, gathering the memory. "So, you didn't want to sell it? I don't believe we've ever discussed that…you hid it well."

"Of course I didn't want to sell it," Todd replied, annoyed, frustrated. "It was the nicest car I had ever owned. It's still the nicest car I ever owned."

"So, why did you sell it?"

"I couldn't afford the damn insurance," Todd said, remembering the entire situation like it was new.

"Did you try to change it…the insurance?"

"Of course…but.."

"But…your mother was involved…somehow?"

"She was on the title of the car," Todd explained. "I had to have her permission to change the policy…to lower the price."

"And she wouldn't give you that permission?"

"No."

"So, what did you do?"

"I tried to take my mother down to the insurance place," Todd explained. "I wanted her to change the policy to something I could afford...so I could keep the car. I thought everything was going fine...until the lady explained what the policy was."

"Basic?"

"Yes," Todd replied, annoyed, even after all the years. "My mother said she wouldn't sign it. I had wasted the whole fucking day...just to have her say no at the end."

"So, what happened?"

"I got mad," Todd laughed. "I got real fucking mad, probably madder than I had ever been at her."

"Why?"

Todd shook his head, angry with the memory of it all. "She didn't care about me," he explained. "She wasn't concerned about me...she was just hung-up on the car, the fact that it had been a gift from my grandfather...her father. That was all she cared about."

The demon hesitated for a moment, seemingly thinking about everything that Todd had just said...then it looked at Todd. "Tell me, did your mother know that you wanted to move out...that that was the reason you wanted to lower the insurance price?"

The question hit Todd hard...it had haunted him for years. "I don't know," he replied, honest. "I really don't know. I had mentioned it...that I wanted to leave...but I really don't know."

"This all happened...after her father died...your grandfather?"

"Yes."

"This was after her husband...your father, had left her?"

"Yes."

"And now...you were threatening to leave?"

"Yes."

"But you believe the whole reason that she would not let you change the policy was due to the fact that it was a gift...the car?" The demon asked, dubious...knowing.

Todd hesitated, but then nodded his head, yes. "I...think so," he finally replied.

"You...think so?"

Todd sighed. "I thought it was all about the car...my grandfather...at the time," he then replied, sounding anything but sure.

"But then it became something else?"

"It was years later," Todd began, remembering something else. "My mother and I had another argument."

"About?"

Todd laughed at that simple question. "God knows," he then replied. "I really don't know what started it. Probably something about me not helping around the house. That was something she loved to start shit with me about in those days."

"Oh really?" The demon asked, feeling this was something else…something new. "Did you help around the house? I don't remember us chatting about that subject before."

"No, not really," Todd replied, honest.

The demon laughed. "Guess we will discuss that at a later time…I feel a certain pain in the subject."

Todd rolled his eyes.

"Go on," the demon pressed, dropping the subject of helping around the house…for now.

"During our argument," Todd continued, "my mother started to talk about how she had lost…"

Suddenly a memory escaped Todd's mind, one that even surprised him.

"Well," the demon said, excited, taking in the escaped memory, "that's a good one."

Todd sighed, pushing back the memory, annoyed that it had gotten away. "Anyway, she was talking about all the things she had lost, her father, her husband, her home, and then she said it…"

"What?"

"That she had lost me," Todd replied.

"How did that make you feel?"

"Uncomfortable," Todd replied. "I quickly turned it around and reminded her that I had also lost those things…including a mother."

The demon looked at Todd, expecting more. "You said it made you feel…uncomfortable…but that's not true…is it?"

Todd shook his head, no. "I really didn't feel anything…not really. I was only saying what I wanted her to hear…so I could leave and not deal with all again later…so she would stop talking."

"Did she?"

"Yes, but she acted like we had just had some amazing breakthrough," Todd explained, remembering.

"Did you…have a breakthrough?"

Todd again shook his head, no. "It was all a lie…I only said it all to shut her up, to end an argument."

"What happened next?"

"I called a girl to come get me…so I could get the hell out of there."

"A girl…what girl?"

"Shauna," Todd replied.

The name instantly brought up an assortment of hidden pains, terrible memories…and multiple failures.

The demon laughed, feeling the wide variety of pains that the name caused.

"One of my favorite subjects," it then said, practically drooling at the thought of launching into the subject of Shauna.

"No," Todd quickly said, shutting the demon out entirely on that subject. "Not tonight...not about that."

The demon laughed.

---}

"Fine," the demon laughed, sitting down, changing forms, now back in its own terrible for. "We can talk about Shauna another time. I do love how upset you get about that subject though."

Todd gave the demon an angry look.

The demon laughed. "Oh, very well, let's get back to your mother...there is deep pain there too. Tell me...about the day you moved out."

"We had just moved into the shitty little trailer," Todd began again, "when we drove up to the house...to get my stuff."

"What happened?"

"My mother walked out," Todd explained.

"That couldn't have gone well," the demon laughed. "What did she say?"

 Todd thought for a moment, poking at the fire as he did so. "She told me that I could take back the Jeep that I had bought…that I could still go get my car back…that was all she cared about…the car."

"Is that true…could you have gotten it back?"

 "No," Todd replied, finding the question rather dumb. "That's not how used car lots operate. I never saw the car again…it was gone."

"How did she handle that?"

"She was heartbroken," Todd replied, despite how terrible it was.

"Then what happened?"

"I started putting my things in the Jeep," Todd replied. "I, uh, think that was the first time that she really realized that I was leaving."

"And what did she say?"

"I really don't know," Todd replied, feeling that he was being honest. "I just tried to load whatever I was taking with me as quickly as I could."

"But something happened?"

"When I brought out the pieces of the bed, the frame…she suddenly lost it."

"Lost it? What did she do?"

"She said I couldn't have it."

The demon gave Todd a sideways look. "That doesn't sound so bad," it then said.

"She grabbed ahold of it," Todd continued, then she said something about me needing to go clean my room…like I was a child."

The demon laughed. "Did you…go clean your room?"

"No," Todd replied, then seemed to sink within the memory. "I tossed it on the ground…and left. I never spent another night in that house…where I grew up."

"So…you left your mother…all alone, after all she had gone through?"

"Yes," Todd replied. "For Gwen."

The demon laughed.

--}

Chapter 6.

There was a brief silence. The demon sat across from Todd, running its hands through the flames of the fire, its eyes fixed on Todd. For his part…Todd sat completely still…and completely silent. If the demon wanted anything else that night…it would have to work for it.

Finally, after about 10 minutes of complete silence…

"So, how was living together…in that trailer?" The demon finally asked, breaking the silence.

"Awful," Todd replied, honest. "From the very start…we had serious issues."

"Problems?"

"From day 1, I had a feeling that Gwen was only going to be there for a little while," Todd explained, "that at any minute…she might leave."

"Trust issues?" The demon laughed. "I can understand that…considering the past that you two shared."

"It was more than that," Todd replied. "Mostly, I just figured she would leave…when the money ran out."

The demon nodded its head that it understood. "Money…the destroyer od all things."

"We had a small, 5,000-dollar nest egg," Todd explained. "To me, back then, that was a fortune."

"Sounds like a decent start," the demon replied. "At least there was something.

What happened to it?"

"I pissed it all away," Todd replied, honest, remorseful.

"How?"

"Well, my first mistake was the Jeep," Todd explained. "It wasn't a bad Jeep, not really, but for some stupid reason, I traded it in for a car…then a truck, then another car…some little green piece of shit that never started in the morning."

"And that's where all your money went?"

"No…not really"

"Go on."

"I pissed most of it away on 2 racecars," Todd replied, watching the tip of a stick he was holding burn.

"Racecars?" The demon laughed.

"Yeah," Todd replied, tossing the burning stick into the fire. "I guess some stupid part of me still wanted to race."

"Even after you chickened out?"

Todd didn't like the way that sounded. "I don't know," he replied, shifting around a bit, realizing his feet were getting hot from the fire. "I guess I wanted to prove something to myself."

"Why 2 cars?"

Todd laughed at that, knowing the answer was ridiculous. "I got one for her."

The demon burst out laughing.

"I know," Todd replied, shaking his head. "It was stupid."

"I'll say," the demon chuckled. "So…what happened next?"

"We tan out of money in a month."

The demon tilted its head, feeling something swelling up in Todd's mind. "Something happened then…didn't it?"

Todd nodded his head, yes. "She denied it," he then began, rather uncomfortable with the memory, "but I think she got pregnant."

"You think?"

"I was dumb," Todd began, remembering it all. "One day she suddenly told me she had to go to the doctor…for something. When I asked her why, she conjured up some story about having cancer."

"Hmm, just like that, huh?" The demon asked, sounding dubious. "Sounds…awful."

"I asked her if I could go to the hospital with her…but…"

"But?"

"Her mother and grandmother didn't want me to go with her."

"Sounds…suspicious."

"That's what I thought," Todd replied, nodding his head, yes, "but I was too dumb to put it all together…I was just worried about her…I loved her."

"So, did you go?"

"Yes," Todd replied, getting a little angry now, remembering everything, "but we didn't go to a hospital…not really."

"Where did you go?"

"To some tiny clinic."

The demon's eyes got big…it knew what was coming.

"She had told me…before we went, before I was going, that she required surgery," Todd explained, "but once we were there, and the nurse called her back…she was in and out in about 15 minutes."

"That doesn't sound like surgery."

"It wasn't," Todd replied. "She had an abortion…I was just too dumb to understand what was happening. She did it right under my nose."

The demon gave Todd a look…as if there was more.

Todd saw the look on the demon's face…he knew what was on the demon's mind. "I just wonder if it was mine…" he then admitted.

The demon vanished…

---}

The demon returned after a few minutes, perhaps giving Todd a few minutes to think about things…to allow the pain to sink in.

It loved to do that….

"What happened next?" The demon asked, once again sitting down on the opposite side of the fire, looking at Todd.

"Things completely fell apart after that," Todd replied.

"Tell me about…Wal-Mart."

"Gwen got a job at Wal-Mart," Todd explained.

"To help pay the bills?"

Todd laughed at that. "For her," he then replied. "She was working for her...and only her. Our money was gone, but nothing she was making went to help us...just her."

"What did she spend it on?"

Todd shrugged his shoulders. "I don't know, but nothing ever came to me...or to the house. Her money was her money...and her mother's. For whatever reason, her mother got a bit of it."

The demon laughed. "Keep going," it then said, loving it.

"Well, one day we decided to go for a drive in our piece of shit car," Todd began, remembering. "The thing was a complete piece of junk, just something with wheels that I had spent my last few pennies on to get to work."

"What happened?"

"The tire popped," Todd replied, remembering.

"Doesn't sound that bad," the demon replied. "I mean, tires pop all the time, right?"

"True, but this car didn't have a spare," Todd explained.

"Ok, so no spare…what did you do?"

"Well, oddly enough, we happened to be right in front of some used car place that sold tires when it popped," Todd explained.

"So, you bought a new tire…or a new…used tire?"

Todd thought about it for a minute, then looked at the demon. "I had 17 dollars on me," he then began, serious, filled with pain. "It was the only money I had left. I had spent every penny on us and would have done anything for that girl…but when I asked her for a few dollars to help get a tire…she wouldn't give me a dime."

"Ouch," the demon laughed. "She had to of been just as screwed as you were though. How would she have gotten home without a tire on the car?"

"Oh, she could just call her mom to come get her," Todd replied, angry, remembering. "Her mother was pushing hard for her to move home by then…she would have come in a minute, then spent the whole ride home, without me there, she wouldn't have given me a ride, telling Gwen all about what a piece of shit I was."

The demon laughed again. "So, what happened?"

"The guy sold me some junk tire," Todd explained, "something that didn't even fit the car. It made the car look freaking ridiculous, up on one side, one corner."

The demon laughed hard.

Todd let the demon stop laughing, then began again. "This was also the time that she started talking about some guy at work. I don't remember his name, just some prick selling phones at Wal-Mart."

The demon gave Todd a knowing look...it had heard this story before.

"I knew right away that something was happening," Todd explained. "I was basically starving by then...my hair was long and dirty looking, but Gwen was doing just fine. Every night, her mother would come get her for dinner...but I was never invited."

"You weren't invited?"

"Nope," Todd replied. "Her mother was trying to get rid of me...even if it meant me starving to death...but there was more to it. While I was at work...Gwen was going out...with the clown from her job...I just never knew it."

"I see," the demon replied. "So, what happened next?"

"I should have known it was over," Todd began, sad. "I don't know, maybe I did and just didn't want to admit it...to be all alone. I wasn't me anymore, she had taken everything from me. The very last day we were a couple...I was going to a friend's birthday party."

"Go on."

"Well, when I got back from that party, I was supposed to go with Gwen...to some dinner party, something dumb her mother was doing...but..."

"But?"

"Her mother said that while I was there...I was not to touch Gwen, to kiss her, touch her, hug her...nothing. She didn't want us to look like a couple."

The demon laughed. "That sounds ridiculous."

"It was...and it pissed me off."

"How mad did you get?"

"Well, when Gwen's mother came to get her, you know, taking every opportunity to have her with her...at home...her home, Gwen tried to kiss me..."

"Go on."

"I guess she was she was just giving a kiss to say…see you later…or something, but…"

"What happened?"

"I pushed her away…with my hands…and a foot…I guess…I had just had enough."

"What did she do?"

"She tried to smack me," Todd replied, sad-like, "but I pushed her away again…then she left the trailer…crying. It was the end…but even then…I was a fool."

"Go on."

"Well, when I went to my friend's party," Todd explained, "I looked so bad that people were talking about me like I was the walking dead…just skin and bones. It was awful…but I still tried to have a good time…but I was thinking of her the whole time…even after it all…I still loved her."

"Did you call her?"

"Yes," Todd admitted. "I'll never forget it…ever."

"What did she say?"

"Todd, I've moved out," Todd replied. "While I was gone, her and her bitch mother had loaded up all her stuff…and moved her out…I was alone."

The demon laughed.

---}

The demon sat silent for a few minutes, looking at Todd…waiting for more.

"What more do you want?" Todd asked, perhaps for the first time that night wanting the conversation to end.

"Come now, there is more to this story," the demon quickly replied.

Todd knew what the demon wanted.

"Go on," the demon pressured.

"Well, I remember when I got home, back to that shitty trailer...and found all her things.... gone, how alone I suddenly felt."

"What did you do?"

"I finally broke down...bad," Todd replied, honest, the pain of that night still deep within him. "I remember hitting rock bottom...just sitting in the doorway...crying, shouting over and over that I didn't want to be there...alone."

"But you were...alone?"

"I was..."

"What happened next?"

"Well, the very next morning...I awoke to the sound of something...outside. When I opened the door to see what it was, I found some guy...turning off my power."

"You didn't pay the bill?"

"I did," Todd quickly replied, "but Gwen's mother had convinced her to call the power company and have it turned off. That's how much of a bitch she was."

"Wow," the demon chuckled. "She really hated you. So, what did you do then?"

"I drove straight to her house, where Gwen was now living, and confronted her about it," Todd explained. "She told me all about it, what her mother had told her to do."

"Go on."

"So, I asked her, begged her really, to come with me, hoping she s=could get it turned back on," Todd explained. "I was young and dumb and didn't understand how shit worked."

"Did she go with you?"

"Yes," Todd laughed. "She had told her mother that I had kicked her, and that I was dangerous, but there she was…the very next day, going out with me."

"Doesn't sound like she was all that scared of you."

"No, she wasn't," Todd replied. "her mother had used the fight to her advantage, to get her away from me once and for all." Todd hesitated...there was something more.

"Go on," the demon pressured, knowing.

"Gwen was already fucking around," Todd explained, "with that loser at Wal-Mart...and he was married, so Gwen was just creating another mess."

The demon laughed. "Didn't take long for her to get over you."

"She had actually told me once, that he was trying to touch her, trying to kiss her, that he didn't love his wife anymore...and me being a fool, believed it all, that she was the victim."

"Wasn't she?"

"Oh, I'm sure he was doing those things, he was a piece of shit," Todd replied, managing a little laugh, "but I'm even more sure that she was going along with it the whole time...without question. I'm sure she was sucking him off every night I worked. I was nothing but a fool."

"A fool in love," the demon laughed. "Go on."

"For whatever reason, she had actually showed me where the guy lived," Todd explained. "She made me drive past it one night. I never even asked her to show me…I have no idea why she did it."

"And…what happened?"

"It was a few days later…after we had broken up," Todd began, "and we were supposed to hang-out…or something, I don't exactly remember what we were supposed to do…but I couldn't find her anywhere. Her parents wouldn't talk to me, and she wouldn't answer her phone."

"Where was she?"

"With him," Todd replied, angry a little at the memory. "Deep down, I knew she was with him…somehow. So, I drove over there, hoping I was wrong…but she was there, with him…alone. She had spent the night there."

The demon laughed. "With him and his wife?"

"She had spent the entire day with him," Todd explained, "then the majority of the night, right up until his wife came home, then, the minute she left, she came back. Hell, I think she slept in his car until it was clear for her to come back in. They had been fucking behind his wife's back…behind mine."

"What did you do?"

Todd laughed. "I made a fool of myself," he then admitted, "crying like a bitch, begging her to come with me."

"She didn't?"

Todd scoffed at that. "No, she even lied to the guy, telling him that she didn't know how I found where he lived…then he started acting like some kind of tough guy, like he was a military police officer or something, sticking up for his new little tramp, his secret sex toy…all while she watched, not saying a word."

"What happened?"

"I left," Todd replied. "I left her there…with her married lover…in another trailer…and that was the end of it…it truly ended that day."

The demon stood up, as if stretching. "Such a wonderful story," it then said. "I love the pain that it still brings you…even after all these years."

Todd actually managed a laugh.

"What?" The demon asked, surprised by Todd's reaction.

"It doesn't hurt me anymore," Todd replied. "Shame…yes, but not pain, not anymore…not like you think.”

The demon was dubious. “The story obviously bothers you,” it then said, serious. “I know you told me the truth…but you still shield much of it, secret memories, to this very day. If it isn't pain that you are keeping away from me…what is it?”

Todd laughed, then gave the demon a very strange, almost crazed look.

“Tell me?” The demon asked, suddenly a bit off its guard.

“The truth.”

“What truth?”

Todd hesitated, but then looked at the demon, straight into its eyes. “That I am dead inside,” he then said, and for the first time that night…wounded the demon.

The demon drew back a little, obviously surprised…stunned. “You've never said that to me before.”

“It's true,” Todd replied, now looking back into the flames. “everything that we just spoke of…happened in one year of my life…one year…but my whole cursed life has been one tragedy after another, one continuous trial...and I have failed at every turn."

The demon looked at Todd.... its roll suddenly changed into one it rarely practiced. "No...you have not failed."

Todd, now shocked himself, looked at the demon. "My whole life is one big failure."

The demon shook his head, no. "You have survived...and in the end, in this world of pain, that is all that matters...despite the horrors you have endured...all the pain."

The demon vanished.

---}

Publix...

"We have a real problem!" Bryce barked, sitting behind his desk…safe, where he could pretend to be someone. "You're attitude around here is so negative. It's like you just don't care about the Publix vision!"

I remember laughing at that.

"You think this is funny?" Bryce nearly shouted, making some ridiculous motion to my manager, Sarah, standing behind me, as if I were ridiculous, a fool.

"They asked me for rolls…then came back five minutes later," I explained, ignoring Bryce's dumbass question, despite how ridiculous it was, how it sounded…the Publix vision.

Bryce scoffed. "I know it was a lot more time than that," he then lied. "Those girls worked really hard to get everything ready…and you ruined it."

"I ruined it?" I chuckled.

"Those girls work hard here!" Bryce barked. "They have made Publix their career…and you dropped the ball!"

I held my tongue…somehow.

"I just don't think you see the Publix vision," Bryce said, shaking his head. "In fact, I'm not even sure what you do around here. It's like you just don't care."

I couldn't help but laugh.

"There, you think this is funny again???!"

"I think you are power tripping!" I replied, and all hope of me keeping calm…was gone.

Bryce, shocked, believing he could just talk endless shit to me without me responding, sat back, suddenly nervous.

"Those girls don't do a fucking thing here and you know it," I continued. "They were Joe's pets, you know, before he got sent away for…misconduct."

Bryce's eyes got big…but he didn't say anything. Beside me, Sarah looked at me like I had just killed someone.

"You have no idea how anything works in the bakery, none, and if you think those two bimbos have any clue…well, I don't know what to say…it doesn't speak well of your management skills though."

Bryce sat forward, looking at me. "Well, Todd, maybe…you know, if you ever spoke up…we might be able to get you onboard with things."

I laughed at that.

"There you go laughing again…why?"

"Because it's ridiculous!" I damn near shouted. "I came here on the finalist list and the district manager never even spoke to me, but he promoted some girl who walked around talking about fucking him…is that fair!?"

Bryce didn't say shit to that.

"And what about our new assistant bakery manager?" I continued. "Have you been able to get a complete sentence out of that one? How the hell did she get promoted? How is it that Angelina walks around here all the time talking about giving the district manager blowjobs? Why did Bret tell Kara that she needed to wear spandex to get promoted? Why do teams of idiot girls walk around the store all day doing nothing, talking about how they are next to get promoted? What the hell are they getting promoted for exactly? Tell me, Bryce, what the shit is the Publix vision…do tell!"

There was silence….

"Well, uh, maybe we just need to…communicate more," Bryce said, stupid-like, lost in the moment. "It sounds like you have some issues with Publix. Maybe you would like to speak privately with me sometime…?

--------- The End.

Other Books By This Author...

Citrus County Florida.

A short book dedicated to the county that I grew up in, Citrus County. What did a little county in the middle of Florida, one without any big-name city, have to offer...well, a lot actually. Take a trip back in time as I describe Citrus County...the way it once was...the way it is now, it may just bring back a few memories of your own...no matter what little town you yourself grew up in. At the very least, you might have a few laughs.

Ybor City. When I was a kid, as far back as middle school, all I ever heard about was what a wild ride Ybor was. Growing up in the middle of nowhere, the stories I heard, about girls, girls doing amazing things, awful things, fantastic things, were enough to keep me interested...wanting a taste. Years later, when it came time for me and my friends to make our mark...we took on Ybor, and it was everything that we had dreamed of, and nothing at all like what we expected. Those were Ybor's glory days...those were our glory days. This is our story.

A mad journey consisting of mind-altering drugs, rock and roll, and the horrors of real life lurking just outside, waiting, stalking.

www.ingramcontent.com/pod-product-compliance
Lightning Source LLC
Chambersburg PA
CBHW072103150726
47999CB00005B/1856